mental
health

Attention Deficit Hyperactivity Disorder

Harry Tournemille

Crabtree Publishing Company
www.crabtreebooks.com

Developed and produced by Plan B Book Packagers
    www.planbbookpackagers.com
Author: Harry Tournemille
Editorial director: Ellen Rodger
Art director: Rosie Gowsell-Pattison
Project coordinator: Kathy Middleton
Editor: Molly Aloian
Proofreader: Wendy Scavuzzo
**Production coordinator and prepress
    technician:** Tammy McGarr
Print coordinator: Margaret Amy Salter
Consultant: Susan Rodger, PhD., C. Psych.,
Psychologist and Professor Faculty of Education,
Western University

Photographs:
Cover, p.1: Rui Vale Sousa/Shutterstock.com; p. 4:
Pan Xunbin/Shutterstock.com; p. 5: Sergey Peterman/
Shutterstock.com; p. 6: Ags andrew/Shutterstock.com;
p. 7: Cranach/Shutterstock.com; p. 8: Leeds
N./Shutterstock.com; p. 9 Ansis Klucis/
Shutterstock.com; p. 10: Cheryl Casey/
Shutterstock.com; p. 11: Ilike/Shutterstock.com;
p. 12: Michael Jung/Shutterstock.com; p. 14: Ollyy/
Shutterstock.com; p. 16: Lasse Kristensen/
Shutterstock.com; p. 17: Alexander Raths/
Shutterstock.com; p. 18: Tracy Whiteside/
Shutterstock.com; p. 19: Somchaij/Shutterstock.com;
p. 20: Light Spring/Shutterstock.com; p. 21:
Apollofoto/Shutterstock.com; p. 22: Diego Cervo/
Shutterstock.com; p. 24: Natalia Klenova/
Shutterstock.com; p. 25: 18 Percent Grey/
Shutterstock.com; p. 26: Andrea Danti/
Shutterstock.com; p. 27: Leah-Anne Thompson/
Shutterstock.com; p. 28: Aletia/Shutterstock.com; p. 29:
Elena Elisseeva/Shutterstock.com; p. 30: Lisa F. Young/
Shutterstock.com; p. 32: Creatista/ Shutterstock.com;
p. 33: Mr. Lightman/Shutterstock.com; p. 34: K. West/
Shutterstock.com; p. 36: Creatista/Shutterstock.com;
p. 37: Ko Studio/Shutterstock.com; p. 38: Claus
Mikosch/Shutterstock.com; p. 39: Aaron Amat/
Shutterstock.com; p. 41: Sergiy N/Shutterstock.com;
p. 42: Stocky Images/Shutterstock.com; p. 43:
Maxx-Studio/Shutterstock.com; p. 44: Nico Traut/
Shutterstock.com; p. 45: Layland Masuda/
Shutterstock.com.

Library and Archives Canada Cataloguing in Publication

Tournemille, Harry, author
    Attention deficit hyperactivity disorder / Harry
Tournemille.

(Understanding mental health)
Includes index.
Issued in print and electronic formats.
ISBN 978-0-7787-0069-2 (bound).--ISBN 978-0-7787-0086-9
(pbk.).--ISBN 978-1-4271-9393-3 (pdf).--ISBN 978-1-4271-9387-2
(html)

    1. Attention-deficit hyperactivity disorder--Juvenile literature.
I. Title.

RJ506.H9T68 2013   j618.92'8589   C2013-906482-6
                                                C2013-906483-4

Library of Congress Cataloging-in-Publication Data

Tournemille, Harry, author.
    Attention deficit hyperactivity disorder / Harry Tournemille.
        pages cm. -- (Understanding mental health)
    Audience: 10-13
    Audience: Grade 7 to 8.
    Includes index.
    ISBN 978-0-7787-0069-2 (reinforced library binding : alk. paper)
    -- ISBN 978-0-7787-0086-9 (pbk. : alk. paper) -- ISBN 978-1-4271-
9393-3 (electronic pdf : alk. paper) -- ISBN 978-1-4271-9387-2
(electronic html : alk. paper)
    1. Attention-deficit hyperactivity disorder--Juvenile literature.
I. Title.

RJ506.H9T5557 2014
618.92'8589--dc23
                                                2013037006

Crabtree Publishing Company

www.crabtreebooks.com   1-800-387-7650   Printed in the USA/052016/JF20160408

Published in Canada
Crabtree Publishing
616 Welland Ave.
St. Catharines, ON
L2M 5V6

Published in the United States
Crabtree Publishing
PMB 59051
350 Fifth Avenue, 59th Floor
New York, New York 10118

Published in the United Kingdom
Crabtree Publishing
Maritime House
Basin Road North, Hove
BN41 1WR

Published in Australia
Crabtree Publishing
3 Charles Street
Coburg North
VIC, 3058

CONTENTS

Attention Deficit Hyperactivity Disorder is among the most common mental health disorders in children and teens. Researchers are learning more about it every day.

Can't Sit Still

"Somedays, if I forget my meds, it's like this, I'm at school at my desk and I can't sit still. Even if I could, I don't know if I'd want to. My brain shoots off like fireworks. Multiplying fractions—who the hell does that? I look at the numbers and they make no sense. Orange. My answer is orange. How's that? I had oranges at breakfast. When was breakfast? It has to be lunch soon. Everything bounces around in my skull like bees in a jar. The classroom smells like feet. The teacher writes on the chalkboard. Everything around me is fighting for the same spot in my brain.

My eyes hurt. There's a constant buzzing sound in my head and there's so much noise. And then I look like even more of an idiot because I say something out loud and everybody hears it."

— Zak, 17.

Recognize That It's Real

Many people struggle to sit still, focus, and pay attention. But Attention Deficit Hyperactivity Disorder (ADHD) is more than just the fidgets. In the past, many of the behaviors that characterize ADHD were thought to just be kids being kids —active, impulsive, and restless. By the 1970s, doctors recognized that this disorder was brain-linked. ADHD used to be called hyperactive, hyperkinetic, or Attention Deficit Disorder (ADD). Researchers thought ADD and ADHD were separate disorders. Now, ADHD is considered one disorder, with different **presentations**. It is the most frequently diagnosed neurobehavioral disorder in kids. ADHD is also classified as a **psychiatric** disorder.

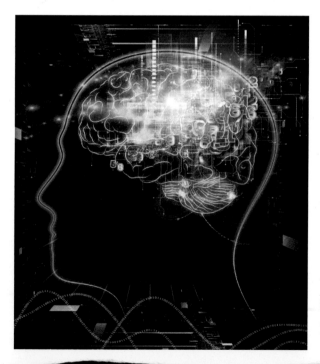

It Feels Like...

Children, teens, and adults with ADHD struggle to handle all the information racing through their heads. A massive amount of energy is required just to focus on one particular thing. Some people "hyperfocus" — meaning that they spend too much time focusing on one thing.

A neurobehavioral disorder relates to how the brain effects behavior, or the way we act, as well as learning and emotions.

It Doesn't Have to Be Scary

The term "psychiatric disorder" sounds scary but the truth is, if you have ADHD, you are not stupid or weak or a freak. Your brain simply works differently—and sometimes in a way that's really cool. What's awesome is there are many ways for people with ADHD to not only cope with their hyperactive minds, but to use them to really benefit their lives.

Sometimes we make things more frightening than they really are—like this monster made from a hand shadow.

Even if they force their body to sit still, people with ADHD often feel like their brains are bursting with fragments of information.

8

Chapter 1

What Is ADHD?

ADHD is the short form for Attention Deficit Hyperactivity Disorder, a neurobehavioral disorder in which the brain functions differently, resulting in behavioral, emotional, or learning difficulties. A neurobehavioral disorder is brain-linked, or brain-related. It is connected to the central nervous system (CNS) in the brain. The CNS is like a computer processor. It receives, processes, and sends information from all parts of the body. With ADHD, a person will find it difficult to stay focused or pay attention.

Sometimes Subtle, Sometimes Not

ADHD isn't always something easy to see. Someone with ADHD may not realize they're different until they're in a setting where it's noticeable, such as school, work, or at an event with a group of people. The symptoms may be more noticeable in places where sitting quietly and working on a specific task for long periods of time is required. This sort of scenario often results in acting out behavior. A person with ADHD may blurt loudly, create disturbances in the classroom, grow frustrated, and get up from his or her desk.

Sitting still in school can be difficult with ADHD.

9

"My grades were good but my assignments were always late. Everything about me was late. I could never focus. I'd start on something, do a little of it, then get into something else. And I'd get interested in things, then drop them. I just couldn't get how people could always be on time and always remember things. Even when I wrote things down, I would forget. My mom would get so angry with me."

— Mandy, 15.

Control Yourself!?

When they do act out, a person with ADHD may be told to sit down or shut up. They may get in trouble in the classroom or find themselves seeking out risky behavior because it feels like a release. If you have ADHD, you may get poor test scores or even have to repeat a grade. Then again, you may be pretty good at managing some of your symptoms (or your parents will be good) and, if you are clever, be able to pull off great grades. For some people with ADHD, friends may be hard to make or keep. This constant sense of being in trouble or being different can make someone with ADHD feel **anxious** and frustrated, or act out aggressively. Worse, it can seriously hurt their self-confidence. It can be a lonely way to live.

You're Not Alone

The truth is, if you have ADHD, you are not alone. Statistics show roughly five to eight percent of children (1 in 20) have some form of ADHD, and this carries into their teens as well. This means in any classroom, at any given time, at least one or two students could be dealing with ADHD. So ADHD is pretty common—but it's also specific. Not everyone who feels fidgety in a classroom, or can't focus on an assignment, has ADHD. It's important to be diagnosed.

Signs and Presentations

Researchers who study ADHD have categorized symptoms for determining whether or not someone has ADHD. A symptom is simply an action or characteristic that indicates a person might have ADHD. In diagnosing, children should have six or more symptoms of the disorder and teens and adults at least five.

Symptoms of ADHD fall into three main categories:

- Inattentive presentation: Six or more symptoms of impulsive activity with some tendencies toward not being able to focus.

- Hyperactive-impulsive presentation: Six or more symptoms of inattentiveness (lack of focus or paying attention) with some impulsive symptoms. It will be hard for a person to organize or finish a task, follow instructions, or pay attention to detail. They will be easily distracted and have difficulty remembering routines.

- Combined Inattentive and Hyperactive presentations: Has six or more symptoms from both of the other presentations.

Being impulsive may cause people with ADHD to be risk takers who are prone to more accidents and injuries.

Symptoms

Here are some specific symptoms of ADHD:

Signs of Inattentiveness:
- Frequently switching from one activity to another
- Getting bored with a task after only a few minutes
- Having problems being organized and staying focused
- Losing things (pencils, toys, assignments)
- Not completing or forgetting you have homework
- Seeming not to listen when spoken to
- Daydreaming, moving slowly
- Unable to follow instructions, or taking longer

Signs of Hyperactivity:
- Fidgeting and squirming in their seats; Constantly moving
- Talking nonstop
- Touching and playing with anything in sight
- Unable to sit still at the dinner table or in the classroom
- Problems doing quiet tasks or activities

Signs of Impulsivity:
- Blurting out bad language
- Being impatient, blowing up
- Acting but not caring about the consequences
- Interrupting conversations or other peoples' activities
- Problems waiting your turn
- Showing emotion without holding back

Research shows most people with ADHD have the combined Hyperactive-Impulsive and Inattentive presentations, although the symptoms aren't evident all the time. They come and go, or "flare up."

What Causes ADHD?

ADHD has been around for a long time, and doctors and researchers still don't know exactly what causes it. New research and new discoveries emerge all the time. What we do know is people with ADHD have small changes or alterations that occur in several areas of their brains.

These changes can be genetic, meaning they are passed down from your family, or they can be from environmental causes such as poor health choices or exposure to toxins—or both. It is thought that some environmental causes occur before a child is born, when they are in their mother's womb. Even though these changes in the brain appear small, the impact on the way a person learns and responds to the world around them can seem big.

People with ADHD are also known to be highly creative, capable of pumping out ideas, solutions to problems, and amazing concepts. It's just that they can't always follow the ideas through to a completed project.

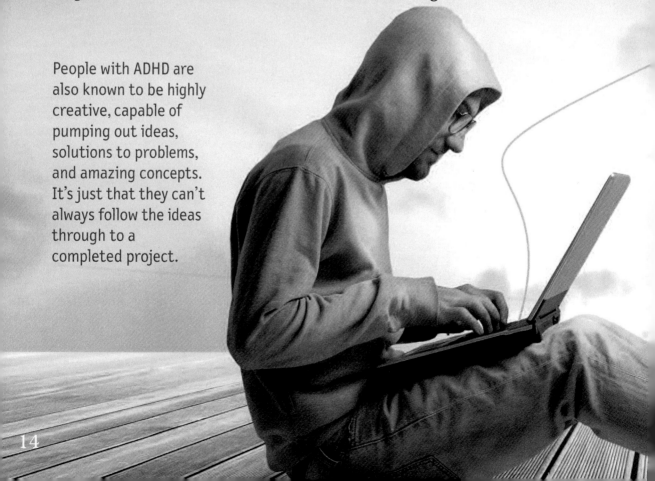

Genetic Factors

Genes are the blueprints that we inherit from our parents. They are the sets of instructions and codes that map out what we are like, including how we look, how we move, how we behave, and how we survive. We all carry thousands of genes in our bodies and researchers are currently seeking out specific ones that determine whether a person could develop ADHD. Doing so would allow them to focus on better treatments and medications, or find a way to prevent the disorder.

Recent Research

A recent discovery revealed that children with ADHD, who also carry a particular version of a certain type of gene, had thinner brain tissue in the areas of the brain associated with attention. This was not a permanent trait, however. As the children grew, so did the gene. Eventually the brain developed to a normal level of thickness and ADHD symptoms also improved. According to another theory, ADHD may be an evolutionary response to the changes in technology, pace, and stimuli (things we respond to) in our world. According to this theory—which has not been proven yet—people with ADHD may be ahead of the curve because they have the short attention spans required to navigate our digital world of the Internet, phone apps, texting, and instant messaging.

The ADHD brain works best when there is no clutter of ideas and things to prevent clear thinking.

16

Chapter 2
Diagnosis and Treatment

The process of diagnosing ADHD is complex and usually requires the help of a family doctor and a specialist. Your parents, your teacher, and even you may sense something different about your behavior. You may reach out to find some answers. The first step to proper diagnosis is gathering as much information as possible. Doctors and specialists may snoop around your life a bit, but in a good way. They're not looking to make judgments.

Some people are diagnosed with ADHD as children, usually when their behavior causes difficulties in school. Others are diagnosed as adolescents or teenagers. Some are diagnosed as adults and still others are never diagnosed because their symptoms are brushed off as something they can control themselves if they "just tried harder." But mind power alone isn't going to change ADHD. Seeking help for your symptoms isn't a sign of weakness—it's a sign of strength and self-knowledge.

ADHD is a condition that needs medical and behavioral help from doctors and psychologists.

"I watched a news special on students taking ADHD meds to do better in school to get an extra 'edge.' I thought they had found us something to help 'even the field,' but now there's a whole bunch of people out there trying to gain more ground than we get with them. One kid said he steals them from his little brother and he doesn't know it and I'm like 'bull...unless he's a little kid, we know how many 'days' we have left."

—PJ, 18

Seeing a Doctor

Seeing a doctor is the first step to diagnosis. Most doctors, and especially psychiatrists, or doctors who specialize in the diagnosis and treatment of mental disorders, are trained to recognize the many symptoms of ADHD. When you see a doctor, they will ask you questions to determine how your mind works and what symptoms you have. They'll be interested in what makes you happy and what makes you angry. They may ask for examples of when you feel the most anxious, frustrated, or relaxed. They may ask you to keep a journal of your own observations and behaviors. They may ask about what foods you eat, or what your sleeping habits are like. The information they need has to be found from your daily life before they can diagnose and look for ways to help.

What Makes Diagnosis So Tricky?

Even if you show some symptoms of ADHD, there can be many different reasons for the symptoms. So, while a teacher or parent may be concerned about hyperactivity or constant disruption in the classroom, the steps to diagnosing ADHD have to be thorough. This means eliminating other possible causes such as other medical conditions or typical behavior for your age group. Not terribly simple, is it? Think of it as a pile of puzzle pieces in a heap on the floor. The pieces belong to several different puzzles but look similar enough to confuse you. You may think the piece in your hand belongs to one puzzle, when it actually belongs to a different one. The important part is taking the time to make sure you find the right place for that piece.

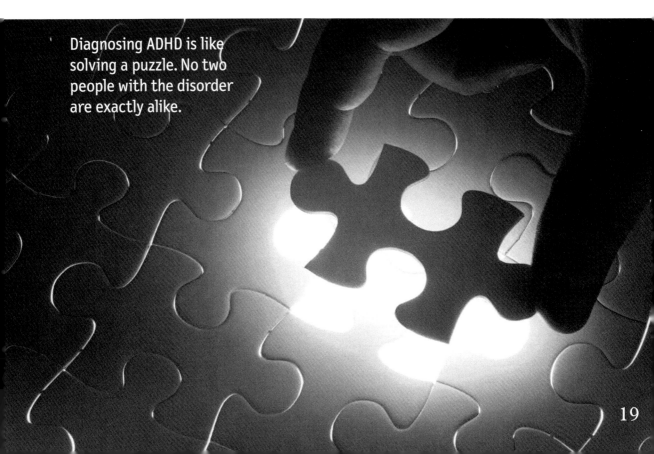

Diagnosing ADHD is like solving a puzzle. No two people with the disorder are exactly alike.

19

Can It Be Something Else?

Typical adolescent and teen behavior can be confused with ADHD, and so can other medical conditions. When diagnosing ADHD in youths, doctors have to rule out other possible medical conditions that have similar symptoms. Some of the health conditions specialists need to rule out are learning disabilities, vision or hearing problems, other neurobehavioral disorders, and stress. When a doctor rules out other possible causes for your symptoms, they will note your symptoms, how long you have had them, and how they affect your life, such as your ability to complete tasks and do well in school.

Not many questions are answered with one visit to the doctor's office. Sometimes you have to wait awhile before finding out the answers.

Okay, So Maybe It Is ADHD

Here's an ADHD math problem: If you have four pencils and seven apples, how many pancakes will fit on the roof? The answer: Purple, because kittens don't share cutlery.

This makes perfect sense to many people with ADHD. The enormous amount of details going through their head at any given time is one thing. Putting these details into working order is another. The ADHD brain jumps from impulse to impulse. It wants to go in 20 different directions at once. Here's the kicker: you can't solve ADHD on your own. No one can. It requires help.

ADHD is a medical condition, not a part of your character. You should also know it's fairly common, but requires a specific diagnosis before treatment. You didn't get ADHD because you were weak or selfish or undisciplined. You got it most likely from your **genetics**, or the environmental influences before your birth.

You should also know your symptoms can be lousy one week and pretty good the next—and they will not go away on their own. Girls can show symptoms differently than boys and be more difficult to diagnose. A boy may be more likely to act out disruptively in a classroom. A girl may be quiet and focused on trying to control their behavior so that they don't call attention to themselves.

What Treatments Are Available?

If you've been diagnosed with ADHD, the most common treatments begin with a combination of medication and behavioral therapy. While both offer different areas of help, doing one but not the other tends to not be ideal. Meds won't do it alone and neither will behavior therapy.

Many studies show regular social **interaction** with proper behavior skills boost happiness. Studies also show that some doses of medication enable people with ADHD to actually seek out social opportunities with friends. The two appear to go hand-in-hand. In many cases, medication is introduced with behavior therapy at the beginning— because meds work quickly. Behavior therapy takes time.

Sometimes meds need to change because they don't work. Meds and behavior therapy work the best to control symptoms and allow people to live normally.

Behavior Therapy

Behavior therapy plays a big role in helping you be responsible for your own behavior. It's a big commitment, often involving teachers, parents, and doctors—but the payoff is it enables you to form real relationships with people, get along better with family and friends, and recognize when you're acting inappropriately.

Therapies usually fall into two main categories:

- **Antecedent Focused Behavior Support:** Rules, routines, and structure set in place to keep you on track. You'll find areas of the house or classroom designed for you to get tasks done, to have quiet space, or to unleash your creativity. Your days will be organized and consistent, and those helping you will also provide a ton of positive feedback on your specific efforts.

- **Consequence Focused Behavioral Support:** Rewarding specific good behavior and recognizing consequences when it does not follow established rules. Goals are set, such as a list of daily chores at home or school. If you achieve them, you get rewarded and new, more challenging goals are put in their place. It helps you mark your own improvement over time.

ADHD and Other Disorders

Sometimes ADHD comes with other disorders. When this happens, doctors call it a comorbidity because two or more disorders occur at the same time. It can be common to have ADHD as well as anxiety and obsessive compulsive disorder, depression, bi-polar disorder, Tourette's syndrome, conduct disorder, or oppositional defiant disorder (**hostility** and **defiance** toward authority). Sometimes people with undiagnosed ADHD will use street drugs to help them cope. The most commonly used are methamphetamine, cocaine, and MDMA. Street **stimulants** may feel like they help calm the ADHD brain, at least at first. Over time, people who take these drugs may develop an addiction, which can further confuse diagnosis and treatment. That's long-term pain for a seemingly short-term gain.

Scientists are not sure if comorbidity disorders are the cause of ADHD, or if they have presented themselves because of ADHD. They do know additional disorders make ADHD symptoms more difficult to manage—especially if you're trying to do it on your own. But doctors treat each patient's symptoms instead of the disorders. This makes treatment individualized and more likely to work.

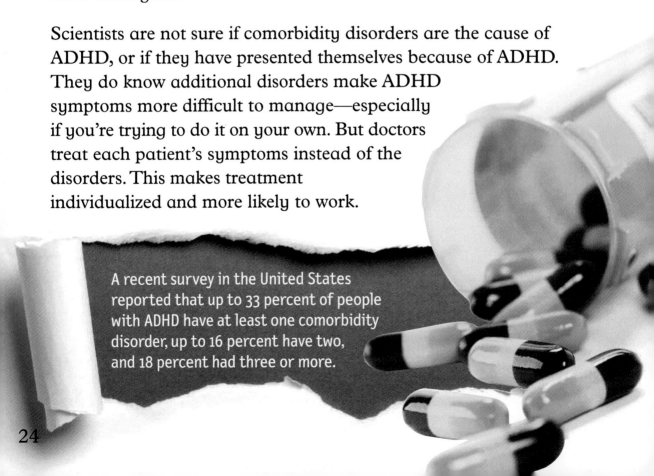

A recent survey in the United States reported that up to 33 percent of people with ADHD have at least one comorbidity disorder, up to 16 percent have two, and 18 percent had three or more.

ADHD and Meds

ADHD medications—also called stimulants—are known to be among the safest of all psychiatric drugs. They tend to work well but like all prescription drugs they have some side effects such as headaches. The meds stimulate parts of the brain associated with attention and decision making by boosting two important neurotransmitters, or chemical messengers, found in the body: dopamine and norepinephrine.

The three most common ADHD stimulants are known by the pharmaceutical names Adderall, Ritalin, and Dexedrine. When taking meds, accurate dosages are important, as is proper diagnosis. Studies have shown problems with dosages set too high, or a misdiagnosis leading to unnecessary medication. Always ask questions and be honest with your doctors. Stimulants are not a cure. You still have to work hard. Stimulants are effective when used as prescribed, but are dangerous when abused.

REMEMBER: No two people are alike so doctors may have different medications for you than for someone else you know who also has ADHD. It's also important to take your meds exactly as your doctor tells you to—at the right times and in the right amounts.

Stigma is serious. The fear and shame of a diagnosis can prevent people from seeking treatment—which only makes things worse.

Chapter 3

Dealing With Stigma

You'd think life gets easier once you've been diagnosed with ADHD and are on a treatment plan. In a sense, you're right. Treatment will help you feel more in control of your life. But life gets tough sometimes. Most adolescents and teens are concerned with how other people see them. Everybody wants to fit in with their peers and be accepted and liked. It's no different for someone with ADHD.

This can be especially difficult for girls, where acceptance can be so important. You want people to like you, and you find yourself doing anything to get that acceptance. Boys do this too, but the feeling of rejection can be a lot more intense for girls. It can be difficult when you make friends but you don't interact the way your friends do. Go easy on yourself. Remember it's not your fault. But this is who you are—and you're not alone. A lot of your frustration is due to others not understanding ADHD. People are the most judgmental about things they do not understand. And not understanding something can lead to **stigma,** or shame.

It's wrong to judge people's behavior before you know their situation.

27

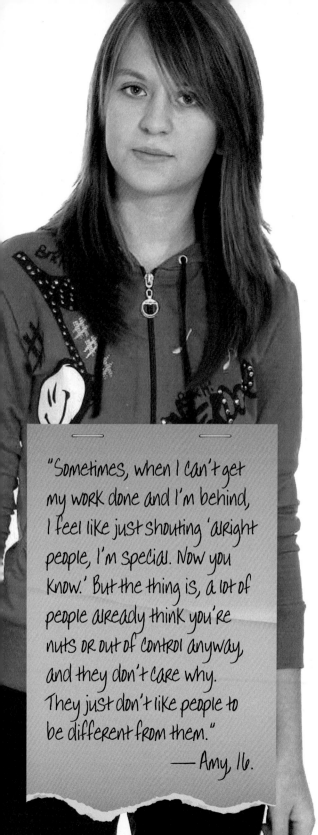

"Sometimes, when I can't get my work done and I'm behind, I feel like just shouting 'alright people, I'm special. Now you know.' But the thing is, a lot of people already think you're nuts or out of control anyway, and they don't care why. They just don't like people to be different from them."
— Amy, 16.

Stick It to Stigma

People tend to fear what they don't know—especially if it makes them uncomfortable—and this leads to **ostracizing** and rejecting people. They see only the actions they can't explain, such as the kid who slams his books on the floor or yells in class. They don't get it.

Having ADHD can be a tough burden to carry, but you have to remember to not let labels prevent you from getting the help you need and from being the person you are.

Being a Friend

Friends are a big deal to a person with ADHD. It's important to know how alone some people feel—and how different. A person with ADHD often feels misunderstood. They do not choose to act the way they do. They act that way because of a medical disorder—and that can be a scary world to live in.

Understanding Makes a Difference

Imagine a classroom or a community where everyone knew about a fellow student's ADHD, and knew why he or she acted a certain way. What if people knew how difficult it was for a person with ADHD to get their thoughts organized and how frustrated they felt by it all. They can feel worthless. Think how much better it would be for everyone if people with ADHD felt as though they belonged and as though they mattered. Think about how this help would improve their lives by relieving stress and anxiety. This is crucial for someone with ADHD—that they understand that they matter. Learn about ADHD and be educated, and try not to joke that every bad decision or move a person makes is "an ADHD moment."

Driving is important to some teens, but it can be difficult for teens with ADHD as it requires sustained concentration and focus.

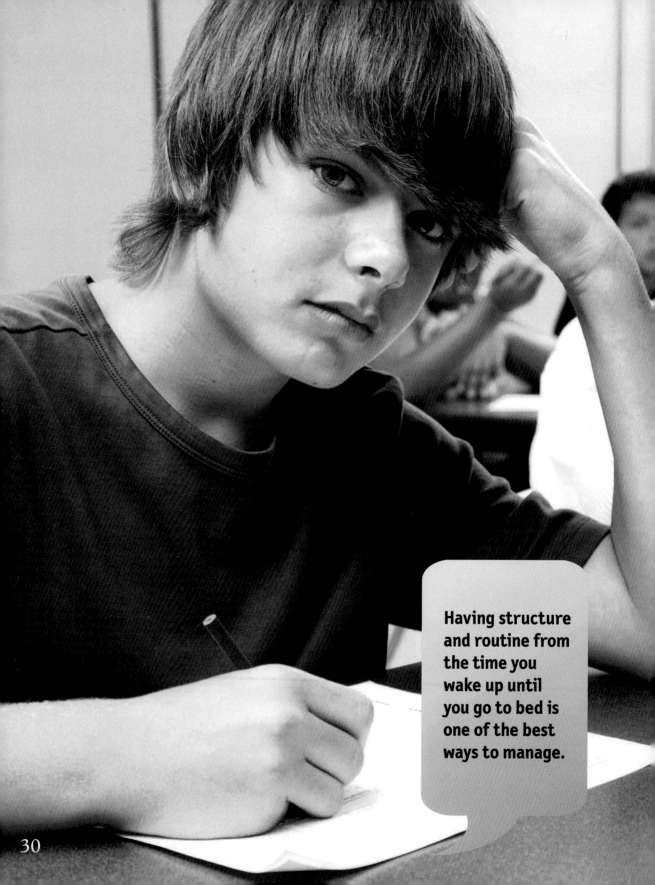

Having structure and routine from the time you wake up until you go to bed is one of the best ways to manage.

Chapter 4
Managing Behavior

Getting your behavior under control requires working with others. For it to work, it will mean communicating with your teachers, your parents, your therapists, and friends. It may also require different methods, depending on who you are and how your ADHD presents itself.

Have a Plan: For instance, if you're at school, you may want to have an agreement with your teachers about taking small, frequent breaks when you feel yourself getting amped up or distracted. Maybe you can have a signal such as holding a pencil up so the teacher knows you require space. They will prefer this to having the rest of the class disrupted.

Routine: One of the biggest aids you'll find in controlling your ADHD is learning how to manage your behavior with routines. These are usually created with your parents, teachers, and counselors, and involve trial and error. None of it will happen overnight. It takes time…and—wait for it—patience.

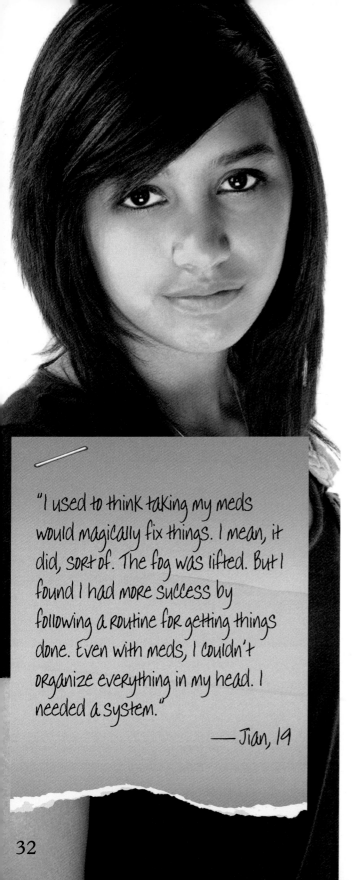

"I used to think taking my meds would magically fix things. I mean, it did, sort of. The fog was lifted. But I found I had more success by following a routine for getting things done. Even with meds, I couldn't organize everything in my head. I needed a system."

—Jian, 19

Brain Overload

Routines are so useful because they keep your brain from overloading. You begin to understand an organized pattern for each day: when to get up, eat, get dressed, and take your meds.

Routines also incorporate times of activity and times of quiet. Each part of the day is broken down into specific tasks, which are a lot easier to manage than random surprises. Some places will have more distractions than others. A busy classroom where people are working in groups and talking loudly may require a lot more effort on your part than sitting at a table at home, working on an art project. You need to know it's okay to be in both environments, but you will have to be more self-aware in one than the other.

What Every Good Routine Needs

CONSISTENCY: It's important to keep daily and even hourly routines. The longer you maintain your routines, the more natural they will begin to feel. If you're on medication, take it at the same time every single day.

EXERCISE: A good routine maintains a healthy mind-body balance. Physical activity is important. Exercise releases **endorphins** and eases a lot of tension and stress.

RELAXATION: Equally important is making sure your daily routines incorporate times of quiet and personal space. Studies show that practicing meditation—though not easy for someone with ADHD—can also have long-term benefits in reducing anxiety. If you notice you're getting amped up, try to sit, close your eyes, and regulate your breathing (slow and deep).

SLEEP AND DARKNESS: This is a big one as it's one of the biggest ways the body regulates itself. Your body needs darkness to properly produce **melatonin** to help you sleep. So make sure your room is dark at night.

FOOD: If you eat garbage, you're going to feel like garbage. Focus on eating fresh fruit and vegetables. Try to limit sugar and processed foods that contain **preservatives**, and caffeine found in soft drinks and energy drinks.

Good friends—the kind who like you and don't try to change you—are important. You need friends who accept you as you are.

34

Chapter 5

Making Friends

If have ADHD, you may find it's exhausting and difficult trying to fit in with others. You might get stressed and act out and then people get annoyed. Maybe you barge in on a soccer game and kick the ball way out of bounds. Maybe you speak too loudly or interrupt others. People can see you as being rude or a jerk—even though you're not trying to be. It's a part of your disorder, and it's important others are aware of this.

Making friends isn't just an option in life—it's a necessity. People need to be social—to make friends and be a friend to others. It's also a crucial part of being a teenager. It can seem as important as eating and sleeping. Without friends, a person becomes isolated and stands a good chance of increasing their depression and anxiety. You need to have connections with other people.

Telling People You Have ADHD

One of the great things about people is their ability to understand —so a part of your friend-making may include letting friends know you have ADHD. You don't want to just tell anyone but, if you trust someone and they seem sincere, telling them about ADHD can be a good thing. It enables your friends to know why you act a certain way. Maybe they can even play a part in helping you when things get tough.

Telling Others You Have ADHD

Milder ADHD symptoms can be easier to hide. But if your symptoms are more obvious and likely to put friends off, then you may need to explain your disorder so they understand. There's no question this isn't easy, especially when you already feel as though you're under a microscope. But people can't understand what they don't know. Trust is a big deal. If people seem to be genuine friends, then telling them you have ADHD will go a long way to keeping that friendship. You don't need to tell people who you don't trust, and you don't need to tell anyone you're not comfortable with.

Be prepared for people to have questions when you tell them about your ADHD. They may want to know what it feels like to have ADHD, and how it affects you at home or in private. Some may just say "okay" and continue on.

Trigger Finger

If you have a friend with ADHD, finding a balance can be tricky. It requires patience, flexibility, and honesty. You know your friend is going to respond to certain situations differently than others. At the same time, you also know how important it is for them to feel included, and to feel like they belong. Sometimes this requires a bit of planning.

A friend with ADHD is already aware of how they're perceived by others. They probably don't feel all that great about themselves. Their self-esteem can be shot. They need compliments and encouragement—even though it's likely they won't respond the same way back to you. There will be times when they aren't good friends, but you can't take it personally. It's a part of ADHD.

"When I got diagnosed, I helped a friend get diagnosed too. I noticed he had a lot of the same characteristics I had. I said, you should get tested, it can change your world. Now we help each other understand treatment. It's good to have someone really get you."

—Zane, 16.

37

Chapter 6

Family Ties

Living with someone with ADHD can be difficult. Not only are you caring for someone whose senses feel constantly swamped with information, and who react in appropriate ways, you're also looking for ways to lessen the affect their disorder has on others. Plus, more often than not, everything has to revolve around them. Not just daily routines, but other life decisions too.

Dad has ADHD?

If the person with ADHD is a brother or sister, you can feel like your needs are always second to theirs. Or, maybe one of your parents has ADHD and you feel like they never listen, or never keep their word when they've given it. It's difficult to build trust when this happens, and easy to get angry or feel helpless. Someone with a neural behavioral disorder such as ADHD needs people like you. They need to know they are cared for and that their hard efforts to learn acceptable behavior and focus on tasks are noticed. They need to feel loved by those they trust. It's a big deal, even if they don't always show you the same love back.

Rages can be a part of living with someone who has ADHD.

What about you?

Obviously your life is affected by all this and you don't always have a say in it. You require love and encouragement just like anyone else. What can you do to cope? Remember that ADHD is a mental health disorder. Your family member's behavior, which can be hurtful at times, isn't always voluntary. They are not intentionally being difficult. If your sister with ADHD has an outburst and says something that makes you angry, try to stay calm and not take it personally.

Self-Medicating

Self-medicating, or using alcohol or drugs to help cope with the symptoms of ADHD, is more common than people think. You might have a sibling, or a parent who self-medicates. Chronic alcohol and drug use causes **erratic** behavior, such as angry outbursts one minute and loving attention the next. It can be difficult and frightening living with a person whose behavior is unpredictable. In these cases, it is important to know that you can't "fix" this on your own. It's okay to tell someone you trust such as another relative, a teacher, or a counselor, that you are concerned about your parent or sibling's drug or alcohol use. If you don't have anyone you feel safe to disclose to, try phoning a toll-free help line. The person who answers your call should be able to help you make a safety plan. No matter what, don't give up. Ask for help.

Look After You!

There are things you can do to help you care for your loved one and yourself. Here are some suggestions:

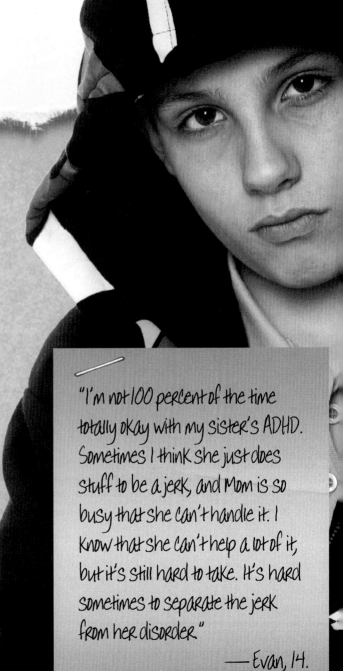

- **Create space. Move to an area where you can regain your calm.**

- **Have "me time" as a part of your daily routine. Even if it's only a half hour.**

- **Breathing techniques—take several deep breaths and let them out slowly. Concentrate on exhaling out bad thoughts, and inhaling calmness.**

- **Go for a walk. Even small amounts of exercise release hormones that calm the body down. A walk can be perfect.**

- **Gather your thoughts. Don't allow yourself to get worked up. Ask yourself if what is making you angry is intentional.**

"I'm not 100 percent of the time totally okay with my sister's ADHD. Sometimes I think she just does stuff to be a jerk, and Mom is so busy that she can't handle it. I know that she can't help a lot of it, but it's still hard to take. It's hard sometimes to separate the jerk from her disorder."

—Evan, 14.

Chapter 7
ADHD Toolbox

Toolboxes—we all know what they are. No, you don't need to go buy one and carry it around with you. An ADHD toolbox should be all the information and skills you have for dealing with your condition. The toolbox is, in essence, your brain, and you're going to pack it full of little tricks and tweaks that will help you through the ADHD rough spots.

This won't be your Dad's toolbox, where everything is a jumbled mess and you have to spend three hours looking for one screwdriver. Your toolbox will be organized—and awesome. An awesomely organized list of coping mechanisms to keep your day going good. Every person's toolbox is different, so remember to keep the tools that work for you and discard the ones that aren't helping.

Pack Your Toolbox

A toolbox can include anything that helps you function in the outside world. Sometimes, it can be useful to have organizers such as notebooks and binders that can help remind you of things you have to do and give instructions on how to do them.

SET GOALS:
Goals can be simple, such as laying out your clothing the night before school or an event. They can also be big, such as setting up your own schedule of school and outside activities. Big or small, simple or less simple, reaching a goal can make you feel good about yourself.

ANTI-DISTRACTION STRATEGY:
Often, people with ADHD find concentration more difficult at the back of the classroom. There can be too many heads to look at, and the teacher is too far away. Try to sit near the front of the class. Use earplugs or headphones to block out sounds when working.

BE PREPARED FOR THE DAY:
Find out in advance about events, tests, and plans, and write them down to make sure that you remember.

KNOCK IT OFF YOUR LIST:
Don't put things off to the last minute. If you have an assignment or test due in six days, work it into your daily schedule so that a little gets done every day. Last minute rushes create anxiety.

FOCUS YOUR FRUSTRATION:
Use a tennis ball, or a small hand-held stress ball, to help you keep fidgeting under control.

HONE YOUR SOCIAL SKILLS:
Learn and rehearse socially acceptable behavior until it becomes normal for use. Develop code signals with teachers, trusted friends, and family so they can remind you when you're acting out.

How NOT to Lose It

Feel like you're about to lose it in class? Have a code word with your teacher that lets them know you need a break. Work on your breathing exercises (in through the nose, out through the mouth). If you have a watch, set a timer so you know when it's time to return to the task at hand. Maybe all you need is 30 seconds, or a minute. Take those breaks so you can continue on.

Communication and Self-Esteem

Never be afraid to express your feelings. There will be days when you feel like everything being said to you is a criticism or that you can't seem to do anything right. If you're frustrated, make sure your teacher, parents, friends, or counselor know. If the criticism comes from people you trust, it's more likely to be a reminder than an attack. But don't hold your frustrations or sadness inside. It messes with your self-esteem and makes you feel anxious.

Communicate when you're having difficulty, when you're feeling jumped on, or when you're happy you figured something out.

Remember Your Value

This may sound silly, but self-esteem is about remembering your value. Whether or not you have ADHD, nobody is great at everything all the time. You will mess up—sometimes daily. This doesn't mean you are worthless or a failure. It means your disorder requires constant work. Acknowledge your mistakes and move on. Allow yourself the room to screw up. Take it easy on yourself and think of the things you are great at: art, or multi-tasking, or soccer, or playing the heck out of your drums.

People won't know what's going on in your head unless you tell them. If your meds are making you feel bad, let an adult you trust know. Talk to your teachers or counselor at school about classroom issues.

45

Other Resources

It can be hard to find reliable information on ADHD. Check your library for books. You can also check the Internet for websites and hotlines that are geared toward your age group. Be careful when searching websites. Not every site gives factual or useful information. Here are some good resources to start with:

Helpful Hotlines
National Alliance on Mental Illness
1-800-950-6264

This is a toll free (U.S.) 10 a.m. to 6 p.m. (EST) national hotline staffed with trained volunteers who can supply information and support for anyone (adolescents, teens, friends, parents) with questions about mental illness.

National Suicide Hotline
1-800-SUICIDE (784-2433)

This toll-free 24-hour national service connects you to a trained counselor at a nearby suicide crisis center. The service is confidential. Also try the National Adolescent Suicide Hotline: 800-621-4000.

Kids Help Phone
1-800-668-6868

A free, confidential, 24-hour hotline staffed by professional counselors. Supports youths who are in crisis and need help and information on a number of issues. Hotline available in Canada only. Visit their website at www.kidshelpphone.ca

Websites

National Alliance on Mental Illness
www.nami.org

This site provides trusted information on mental illnesses such as anxiety disorders, as well as treatment information and where to find support and help. Content is available in English and Spanish.

ADDvance
www.addvance.com

A site with information on teens with ADHD—and especially girls and teens with the disorder. A section on preparing for success in high school gives tips on scheduling, finding ADHD-friendly teachers, and preparing for college.

Mind Your Mind
mindyourmind.ca

An informational teen-oriented mental health site with information on how to get help as well as personal stories about coping, struggles, and successes, a blog, and interactive tools that can help you identify and cope with your mental health disorder.

Teens Health
kidshealth.org

A safe information source on all aspects of teen health, including mental health. Available in English or Spanish.

Teen Mental Health
teenmentalhealth.org

A useful website on a number of mental health topics for youths, their families, and teachers. The site focuses on evidence-based medicine, with trustworthy research articles.

Glossary

anxious Worried, uneasy, or fearful about something

defiance Showing open disobedience or resistance to someone or something

endorphins Hormones in your brain and nervous system that activate the body's opiate receptors, making you feel good

erratic Uneven or unpredictable behavior

genetics Relating to your genes or heredity

hostility Unfriendly or angry behavior

interaction To act in a way that is reciprocal, or to get along with people and have them get along with you

melatonin A hormone secreted by a gland in the brain that helps regulate sleep

ostracizing Excluding someone from a group

presentations The different symptoms of a disorder, or the way it manifests itself throughout a person's lifetime.

preservatives Substances used to prevent decay or rotting in foods and other products

psychiatric Of or relating to mental illnesses and their treatment

stigma Shame associated with a particular illness or behavior

stimulants Drugs that act on the central nervous system and alter brain function, perception, mood, cognition, and behavior

Index